FISH DON'T SNEEZE

There's no such thing as normal.
Be unique. Be different. Be you.

For Mum, Dad, James, Jack & Grace.
Thank you for your unwavering support.
Love you always,

K x

Telltale Tots Ltd.
www.telltaletots.co.uk

First published in the United Kingdom by Telltale Tots Publishing 2020

ISBN: 978-1-9162549-4-7

A CIP catalogue record for this book is available from the British Library.

Text and illustrations copyright © Kirstie Watson 2020

FISH DON'T SNEEZE

Written by
Kirstie Watson

Illustrated by
Nina Khalova

There once lived a fish
who had an unusual problem...

"...A-A-A-CHOOOO!"

He had a bad case of the sneezes.

It was making him very unpopular amongst the other
sea creatures, who had nicknamed him Sneezy.

"Sorry, can't talk now, Sneezy,
things to do!" said one fish.

"Oh, I can't stop... I'm off to play in the scary shipwreck," said another fish.

"Is that the time? Got to go!" said another.

No matter how hard he tried to make friends, no one wanted to play with Sneezy. He felt sad and alone.

"Why doesn't anyone want to be my friend?" he asked one day.

Sneezy jumped when an unexpected voice answered.

"It's because you're different. They don't understand a fish that sneezes. It's not very... normal," said a little fish.

"Oh. But I want to be normal," said Sneezy sadly.

"Don't be sad. I will help find a way to stop your sneezes. I'm Tiny, by the way."

Tiny thought for a moment and smiled.
"Don't worry, I've got a plan!"

"The first thing we can try is quite unusual. You need to
swim up to the surface, pop your head
out of the water **AND** count to ten. Easy!" said Tiny.

"Gulp. I've never done that before," Sneezy said, nervously.
"But okay, if you think it might work."

Mustering his courage, up he swam. Slowly at first, then faster and faster until he could see daylight ahead.

"YOU CAN DO IT!" yelled Tiny from below.

Sneezy took a deep breath, then popped his head out into the fresh air.

He began to count. . .

"1, 2, 3, 4, 5, 6, 7, 8, 9, 10!"

Then he dived back under the sea.

"How do you feel now?" asked Tiny.

"I feel great, and it must have worked because I... A - A - A..."

He sneezed so hard that... WHOOOOOSH! Tiny was
sent tumbling head over fin.

"Oh, it didn't work," said Sneezy, sadly.

"Never mind, I've got another idea," said Tiny.
"The second thing is a little bit silly. But this is what
you need to do... Swim around as fast as you can,
upside down, **AND** count to ten!"

Sneezy felt dizzy at the very thought.

"Don't worry! You've got this!" said Tiny.

Sneezy flipped upside down and swam around as
quickly as he could, counting...

"1, 2, 3, 4, 5, 6, 7, 8, 9, 10!"

"Well, has it worked?" asked Tiny.

"It must have!" Sneezy
replied, "I... **A - A - A...**"

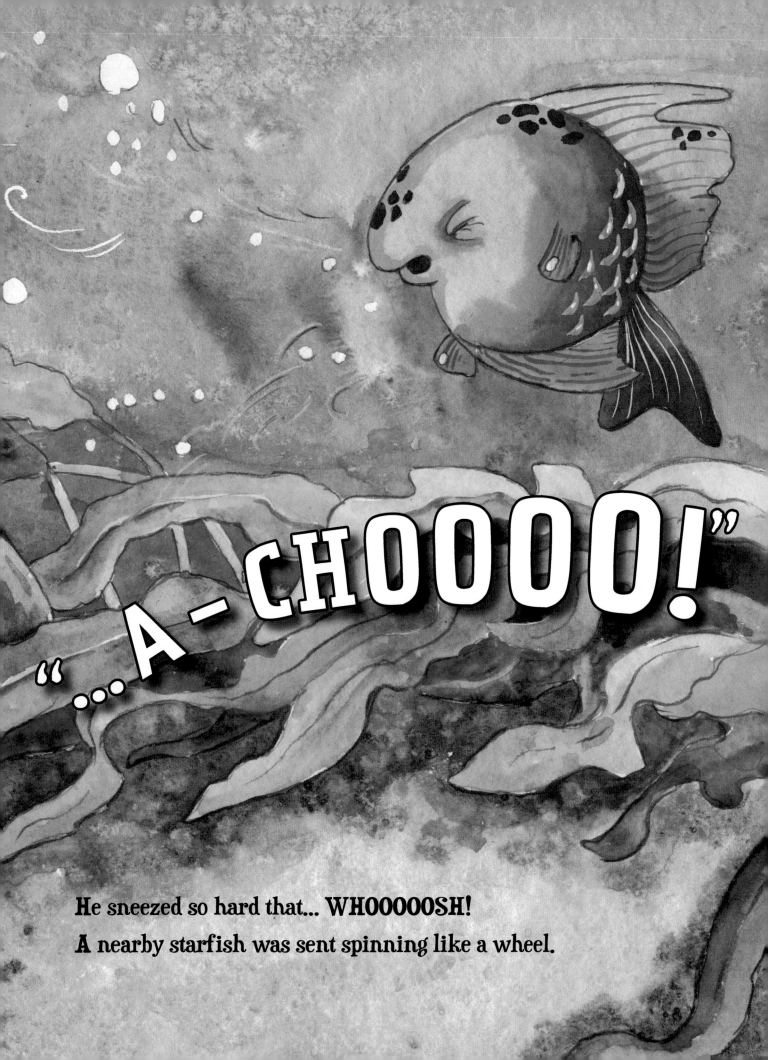

He sneezed so hard that... WHOOOOOSH!
A nearby starfish was sent spinning like a wheel.

"No, that **DEFINITELY** didn't work!" said Tiny.
"But don't fret, I've got one more thing we can try. This will
be frightening, but that's the point. If you want to stop
sneezing, you need a good scare."

"SCARED?! I don't like being scared! But, okay, I'll give it a go."

Sneezy thought for a moment. "The old shipwreck is the scariest place I can think of. Inside are hideous beasts who eat little fish for fun!"

"Perfect!" said Tiny. "You should swim inside, then count to ten! Don't worry, I'll wait outside!"

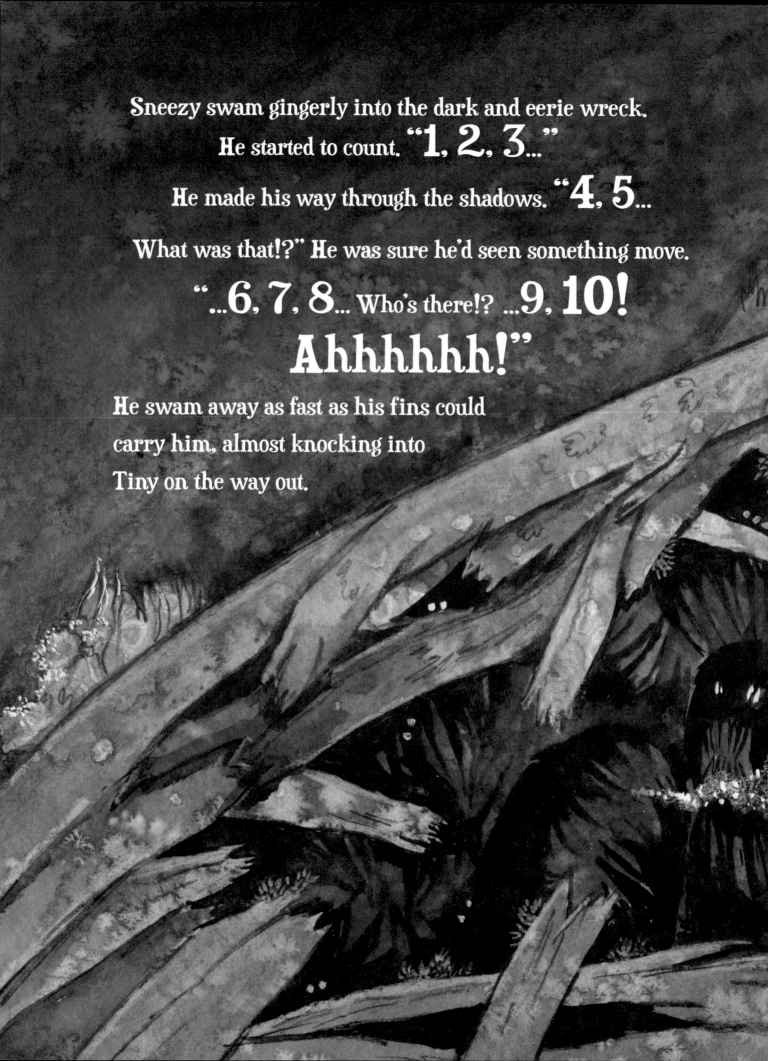

Sneezy swam gingerly into the dark and eerie wreck.
He started to count. "1, 2, 3..."

He made his way through the shadows. "4, 5...

What was that!?" He was sure he'd seen something move.

"...6, 7, 8... Who's there!? ...9, 10!
Ahhhhhh!"

He swam away as fast as his fins could
carry him, almost knocking into
Tiny on the way out.

"Well? Don't keep me guessing.
Has it worked?" asked Tiny.

"I'm not sure. Maybe...
no wait... **A - A - A...**"

"...A-CHOOOO!"

He sneezed so hard that... WHOOOOOSH!
Even the seaweed had to hold on tightly!

"Nothing has worked," sighed Tiny. "I'm sorry I couldn't help you, but perhaps we can try again tomorrow?"

"No, it's okay," said Sneezy.

"Okay?" Tiny asked, "I thought you'd be very disappointed?"

"Me too, but I've had fun today **AND** I've learnt something."
This is who I am. I'm happy being different.
I'm happy being **ME**." he beamed.

"**And** best of all, I found **YOU!** You helped me
when no one else would. You've been there through
sneezes big and small. **YOU** are the greatest
friend a fish could hope for!'"

"We're... **BEST FRIENDS!**" they agreed.

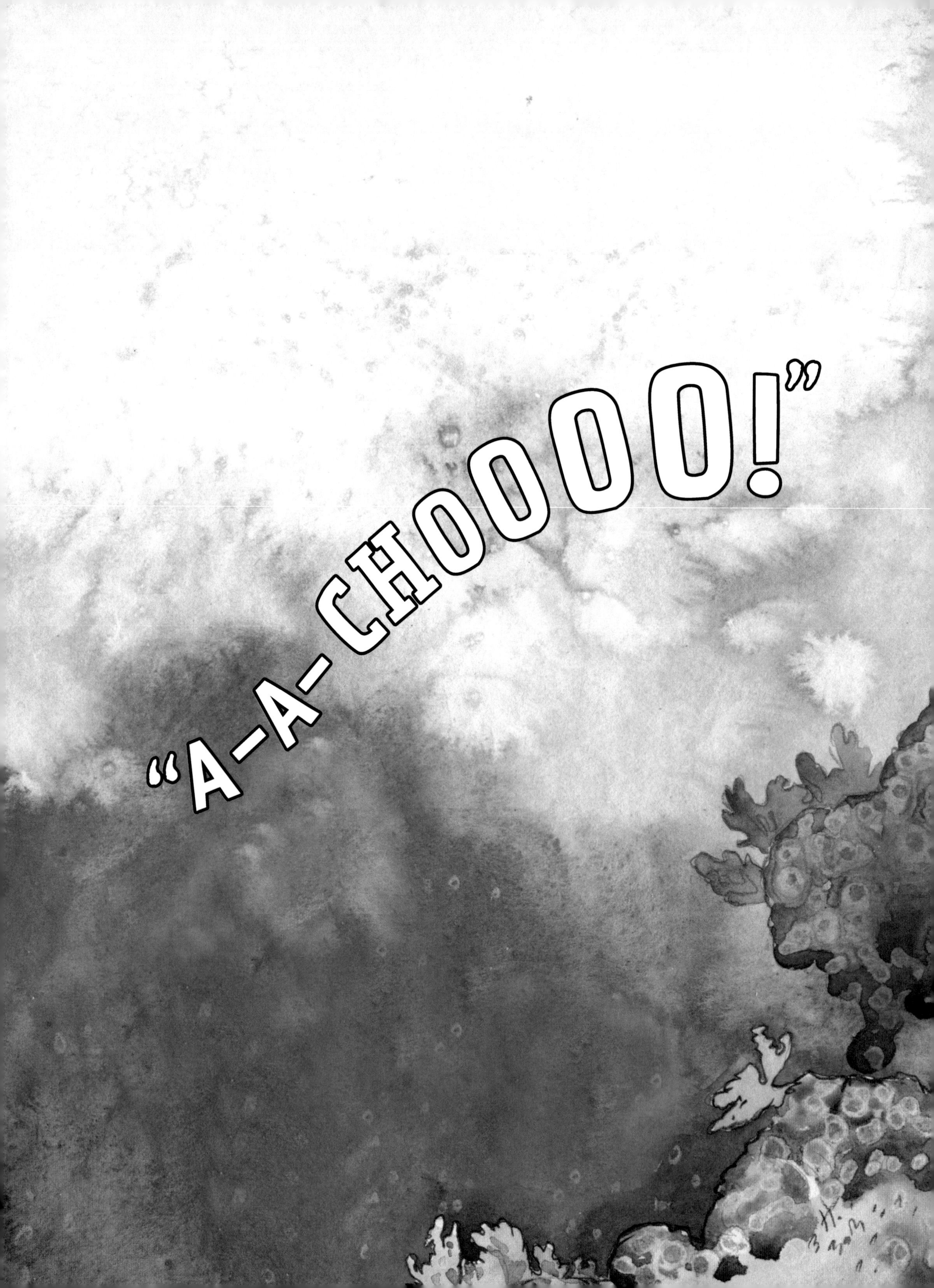
"A-A-CHOOOO!"

The End.

Thank you for buying this book!

Reader reviews are like **MAGIC** for an author like me. They help bring attention to the book, and help others decide if they'd like to buy it too. So, if you enjoyed this book, please consider writing a review.

Kirstie x

Grab a free Fish Don't Sneeze activity pack from:

kirstiewatsonauthor.co.uk/resources

Your book was printed on demand!

This book was printed on demand by Amazon, which helps minimise waste and is considered more environmentally friendly than traditional off-set printing, since books are produced only when they are ordered, reducing the need for large print runs and excess inventory. As the author, I am unable to personally quality check the printed books. However, Amazon provides excellent customer support that you can contact should you have any queries.

Follow me:

facebook.com/kirstiewatsonauthor

instagram.com/kirstie_watson_author

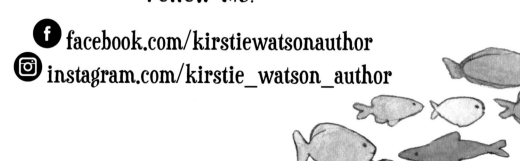

Made in the USA
Middletown, DE
01 March 2024

50675227R00022